Cartel Blo

CW01082694

Chapter 1: The Kingpin Falls

The sun dipped below the Miami skyline, casting long shadows over the bustling port. Containers stacked like giant lego blocks held the city's most lucrative secret. Antonio Brown, the undisputed kingpin of Miami, sat in his office high above the docks, surveying his empire. The port was his playground, and cocaine was the game. Eighty percent of the city's cocaine flowed through here, and Antonio controlled it all with an iron fist.

Antonio was a legend in the streets, a ruthless gangster whose name struck fear into the hearts of even the most hardened criminals. He had built his empire from the ground up, using a blend of charisma, intelligence, and sheer brutality. The Cartel was more than just a business; it was a family, bound together by blood and fear.

In his office, Antonio's sharp eyes scanned the reports laid out on his desk. Shipments were on schedule, money was flowing in, and everything was under control. He leaned back in his leather chair, a rare smile playing on his lips. Life was good.

Down in the port, the night shift was in full swing. Dockworkers moved with precision, unloading cargo under the watchful eyes of Antonio's enforcers. They knew better than to slack off; the consequences were too severe. Among them was Miguel, a loyal lieutenant who had been with Antonio since the early days.

Miguel's phone buzzed, and he glanced at the message. A routine check-in from one of their sources. Everything seemed normal until a series of loud pops echoed through the night air. Miguel's heart sank as he realized what was happening. Gunfire.

In the chaos that followed, Antonio's enforcers scrambled to secure the area. Shouts and screams filled the air as bullets flew, and the once orderly port descended into chaos. Miguel raced towards Antonio's office, praying that his boss was safe.

Antonio heard the commotion outside and instinctively reached for his gun. He stood, ready to face whatever threat had dared to challenge him. The door burst open, and Miguel stumbled in, blood staining his shirt.

"Boss, we gotta get you outta here," Miguel gasped, his face pale with fear.

Antonio's eyes narrowed, and he nodded. Together, they made their way through the back corridors, trying to avoid the escalating violence. But fate had other plans.

As they reached the exit, a figure stepped out of the shadows. The flash of a gunshot was the last thing Antonio saw before everything went black.

The news of Antonio Brown's death spread like wildfire through Miami's underworld. The kingpin had fallen, and the Cartel was left leaderless. Panic and uncertainty gripped the organization as rival factions began to jostle for power.

In the luxurious Brown mansion, Antonio's wife, Maria, sat in stunned silence. Her world had just come crashing down, and she struggled to process the loss. Their daughters, Isabella and Sofia, were equally devastated. Isabella, the elder, had always been groomed to take over the family business, while Sofia had tried to distance herself from the criminal empire.

But the biggest shock came when Maria received a call from a lawyer handling Antonio's estate. There was another heir, a secret that Antonio had taken to his grave. His illegitimate son, Antonio Lewis.

Antonio Lewis was living a modest life in a small town far from Miami. He had always known about his father's reputation but had never been a part of that world. His mother had kept him away, hoping to shield him from the violence and corruption that defined his father's life.

When he received the news of his father's death and the inheritance waiting for him, Antonio Lewis was torn. He had never met his father, and now he was being thrust into a legacy he knew little about. But the lure of the unknown and a chance to understand his roots proved too strong to resist.

Arriving in Miami, Antonio Lewis was immediately struck by the stark contrast between his simple life and the opulence of the Brown family. The mansion was intimidating, and the tension within the family was palpable. Maria and her daughters eyed him with suspicion and resentment, unsure of what role he would play in their lives.

Despite the cold reception, Antonio Lewis was determined to learn about his father and the empire he had built. He met with Miguel, who filled him in on the Cartel's operations and the challenges they now faced. The power vacuum left by Antonio Brown's death had emboldened their rivals, and the Cartel was under constant threat.

Antonio Lewis quickly realized that stepping into his father's shoes would not be easy. He had to earn the respect of the Cartel members, navigate the treacherous waters of family politics, and find a way to unify the organization before it was torn apart by infighting and external attacks.

The streets of Miami were dangerous, and the legacy of Antonio Brown cast a long shadow. As Antonio Lewis began to immerse himself in this new world, he knew he had to be smart, ruthless, and vigilant. His father had built an empire on fear and respect, and now it was up to him to maintain it.

Back at the mansion, Maria watched her stepson with a mixture of fear and hope. She saw in him a chance to restore the Cartel to its former glory, but she also feared that the secrets and sins of the past would come back to haunt them all.

The stage was set for a dramatic power struggle, with Antonio Lewis at the center of it all. The young heir would have to navigate a world of violence, betrayal, and ambition if he hoped to survive and claim his place as the new kingpin of Miami.

Chapter 2: The Secret Heir

Antonio Lewis lived a life that was far removed from the glitz and danger of Miami. His existence was modest, the kind where neighbors knew each other by name, and people left their doors unlocked. He worked at a local mechanic shop, fixing cars by day and spending quiet evenings with his mother, who had raised him alone after leaving Miami and the shadow of his father's legacy behind.

One sweltering afternoon, Antonio was working under the hood of a beat-up sedan when his boss, Mr. Jenkins, called him over. "Antonio, you got a call in the office. Sounds important."

Antonio wiped his greasy hands on a rag and headed inside, curiosity piqued. The voice on the other end of the line was somber and official-sounding. "Mr. Lewis, my name is Mr. Thompson. I'm an attorney handling the estate of Antonio Brown. I'm sorry to inform you that your father has passed away."

Antonio felt his stomach drop. He had always known about his father, the notorious Antonio Brown, but he had never met the man. His mother had kept him away, fearing the dangerous lifestyle Antonio Brown led. "I... I see," he stammered. "Why are you calling me?"

Mr. Thompson continued, "There are matters regarding your father's estate that need your attention. It's imperative that you come to Miami as soon as possible."

The conversation left Antonio in a daze. He finished his shift in a fog, his mind racing with questions. That evening, he sat with his mother at their small kitchen table, the weight of the news hanging heavy between them.

"Mom, why didn't you ever tell me more about him?" Antonio asked, his voice tinged with frustration.

His mother sighed, her eyes weary. "I wanted to protect you, Antonio. Your father was a dangerous man. The world he lived in... it's not a place I wanted for you."

Antonio nodded, understanding but still feeling a pang of curiosity and a need to know more. "I have to go, Mom. I need to see what he left behind. I need to understand."

She reached across the table, gripping his hand tightly. "Be careful, Antonio. Miami is a different world. Promise me you'll stay safe."

With a heavy heart, Antonio packed his bags and boarded a bus to Miami. The journey was long, giving him plenty of time to reflect on the father he never knew and the legacy he was about to step into. The city that awaited him was a far cry from his quiet life, and he felt a mix of excitement and trepidation.

As the bus rolled into Miami, the vibrant, chaotic energy of the city hit Antonio like a wave. He took a deep breath and hailed a cab, giving the driver the address Mr. Thompson had provided. The cab weaved through the bustling streets, eventually pulling up in front of a luxurious mansion. The stark contrast to his modest home was almost overwhelming.

Antonio stepped out of the cab, his eyes wide as he took in the grandeur of the estate. He approached the front door, his heart pounding, and rang the bell. A stern-looking butler opened the door, eyeing him with suspicion. "Mr. Lewis, I presume?"

Antonio nodded, and the butler stepped aside to let him in. The interior of the mansion was even more opulent, with marble floors, crystal chandeliers, and expensive artwork adorning the walls. Antonio felt out of place, like an imposter in a world that was foreign to him.

Mr. Thompson greeted him in the foyer, extending a hand. "Mr. Lewis, thank you for coming. There's much to discuss."

Antonio followed Mr. Thompson into a grand office, where he was introduced to Maria, his father's widow, and his half-sisters, Isabella and Sofia. The tension in the room was palpable, the air thick with unspoken resentment and curiosity.

Maria's eyes were cold as she looked Antonio over. "So, you're the secret son," she said, her tone icy. "Antonio never mentioned you."

Antonio shifted uncomfortably under her gaze. "I didn't know him well. My mother kept me away from this life."

Isabella, the elder daughter, crossed her arms and glared at him. "What do you want? You think you can just waltz in here and take over?"

Mr. Thompson intervened, his voice calm but authoritative. "Antonio has a right to be here. He is part of this family, and he has a stake in the estate. Now, let's all take a moment to process this and discuss how we move forward."

The meeting continued with Mr. Thompson explaining the details of Antonio Brown's will and the responsibilities that came with it. Antonio listened intently, trying to absorb the magnitude of what was being laid out before him. His father had left behind a complex and dangerous empire, and Antonio was now expected to be a part of it.

As the meeting concluded, Antonio found himself alone in the grand office, staring out at the sprawling estate. The reality of his father's world was beginning to sink in, and he felt a mix of fear and determination. He knew that stepping into this legacy would not be easy, but he was ready to face whatever challenges lay ahead.

That evening, Antonio wandered the streets of Miami, trying to make sense of it all. The city pulsed with life, its neon lights and bustling crowds a stark contrast to the quiet town he had left behind. He found a small café and sat down with a cup of coffee, lost in thought.

As he sipped his drink, Antonio realized that this was his chance to understand his father and the world he had built. It was an opportunity to connect with a part of his identity that had always been shrouded in mystery. But it was also a dangerous path, one that could lead to ruin if he wasn't careful.

Returning to the mansion, Antonio steeled himself for the journey ahead. He would need to earn the respect of his new family, navigate the treacherous world of the Cartel, and uncover the secrets that had been hidden from him for so long. The stakes were high, and failure was not an option.

Antonio lay in bed that night, staring at the ceiling. He thought about his mother's warnings and the life he had left behind. But he also felt a spark of excitement, a sense of purpose that he had never felt before. He was ready to step into his father's shoes and claim his place in the Cartel, no matter what it took.

The streets of Miami were calling, and Antonio Lewis was ready to answer.

Chapter 3: Welcome to Miami

The plane touched down at Miami International Airport, and Antonio Lewis stepped off, feeling the heat and humidity hit him like a wall. He had traded the quiet, predictable rhythms of his small town for the chaotic energy of Miami. As he walked through the terminal, he couldn't help but feel like a small fish thrown into a shark tank.

A sleek black SUV awaited him outside, the driver holding a sign with his name. Antonio approached, his duffel bag slung over his shoulder. The driver, a burly man with a stern expression, nodded and opened the door. "Mr. Lewis, welcome to Miami. I'm Carlos. I'll be taking you to the estate."

Antonio slid into the backseat, the cool air conditioning a stark contrast to the oppressive heat outside. The cityscape of Miami whizzed past as Carlos drove through the bustling streets, giving Antonio a glimpse of the world he was about to enter. The neon lights, the crowded sidewalks, and the palpable energy all felt foreign to him.

Carlos finally pulled up to the gates of the Brown family estate. The mansion was even more imposing than Antonio had imagined, with tall iron gates and a driveway that seemed to stretch on forever. As they drove through the gates, Antonio's heart raced. This was it—the world his father had built, the empire he was now a part of.

The SUV came to a stop, and Antonio stepped out, taking in the grandeur of the mansion. The front door opened, and Mr. Thompson, the family lawyer, greeted him. "Antonio, welcome. Come inside, everyone is waiting for you."

Antonio followed Mr. Thompson through the opulent foyer, feeling the weight of the family's history in every piece of art and antique. They entered a grand sitting room, where Maria, Isabella, and Sofia awaited. The atmosphere was thick with tension.

Maria, Antonio's stepmother, was a striking woman in her early fifties, her beauty still evident despite the hard lines of worry etched on her face. Isabella, the elder daughter, looked at him with suspicion, her arms crossed defensively. Sofia, the younger daughter, seemed more curious than hostile, but the air of distrust was unmistakable.

Maria was the first to speak, her voice cold and measured. "Antonio, we've been expecting you. Please, sit down."

Antonio took a seat, trying to maintain his composure. "Thank you. I appreciate you all having me here."

Isabella didn't bother to hide her disdain. "Let's cut to the chase. Why are you here? What do you want from us?"

Antonio met her gaze, trying to stay calm. "I'm here to understand my father's legacy. To see where I fit into all of this."

Maria's eyes narrowed slightly. "Your father never mentioned you. It's hard for us to accept a stranger into this family, especially now."

Antonio nodded, understanding their skepticism. "I get it. I'm not here to take anything from you. I just want to learn about my father and the Cartel."

Sofia, who had been silent until now, spoke up. "What was your life like? Away from all of this?"

Antonio smiled faintly. "Quiet. Simple. My mother kept me far away from this world. She wanted to protect me."

The room fell silent, the weight of their father's secrets hanging heavy. Mr. Thompson cleared his throat. "Perhaps it would be best if Antonio saw the operations firsthand. It might help him understand more about what he's getting into."

Maria nodded reluctantly. "Very well. Miguel will show you around tomorrow. But understand this, Antonio—this world is dangerous. If you're not careful, it will consume you."

That night, Antonio lay awake in the luxurious guest room, his mind racing. He had expected hostility, but the cold reception from his new family still stung. He was determined to prove himself, to earn their respect and find his place in this world. But he also knew that the path ahead would be fraught with danger and deception.

The next morning, Antonio met Miguel, his father's trusted lieutenant, in the grand foyer. Miguel was a grizzled veteran of the Cartel, his face marked by years of violence and hardship. He looked Antonio over, assessing him with a critical eye.

"Miguel," Antonio said, extending a hand. "It's good to meet you."

Miguel shook his hand, his grip firm. "Antonio, let's see what you're made of. Follow me."

They drove to the port, the heart of the Cartel's operations. Antonio watched as workers moved with precision, unloading shipments under the watchful eyes of armed guards. Miguel led him through the maze of containers, explaining the logistics of their cocaine trade.

"This is where it all happens," Miguel said. "Your father built this empire with blood and sweat. If you want to be a part of it, you need to understand every aspect."

Antonio listened intently, absorbing the information. The scale of the operation was staggering, and the risks were immense. He realized that stepping into his father's shoes would require not just understanding the business, but also navigating the treacherous alliances and rivalries that defined the Cartel.

As they toured the port, Antonio noticed the wary glances from the workers and enforcers. They knew who he was, and they were watching him closely. He needed to earn their trust, and that would take time and effort.

Returning to the mansion, Antonio felt a mix of excitement and dread. The world he had entered was dangerous and complex, but it was also a part of his heritage. He was determined to prove himself, to honor his father's legacy, and to find his place within the family.

That evening, as the family gathered for dinner, the tension was still palpable. Antonio took a deep breath and addressed them. "I know it's hard to accept me, but I want to earn your trust. I want to be a part of this family and this legacy. I'm willing to do whatever it takes."

Maria looked at him for a long moment before nodding. "We'll see, Antonio. Actions speak louder than words."

Isabella remained silent, her expression guarded. Sofia offered a small, tentative smile, a glimmer of hope in her eyes. Antonio knew he had a long way to go, but he was ready to face the challenges ahead.

The streets of Miami were unforgiving, and the Cartel's world was even harsher. But Antonio Lewis was determined to navigate this dangerous new life, to earn his place, and to honor the legacy of the father he had never known.

Chapter 4: The Get Money Girls

Lea Torres was a force to be reckoned with. Standing at a striking 5'10", her beauty was disarming, but it was her lethal skills that truly set her apart. Born and raised in the rough streets of Miami, Lea had learned early on that beauty could be both a weapon and a shield. She had carved out a niche for herself as a contract killer, leading a crew of equally formidable women known as The Get Money Girls.

The Get Money Girls were a tight-knit group, each member bringing their own unique set of skills to the table. There was Carla, a tech whiz who could hack into any system; Jasmine, an expert in disguise and infiltration; and Reina, Lea's cousin and right-hand woman, whose sharpshooting skills were legendary. Together, they had built a reputation for being efficient, ruthless, and unstoppable.

On a hot Miami night, the girls gathered at their headquarters, a sleek loft hidden in plain sight above a rundown nightclub. The mood was tense as they prepared for their latest job. Lea paced the room, her mind focused on the details of the hit. The target: the Cartel.

"This one's big," Lea said, addressing her crew. "We've been hired to take down the Brown family's operation. The client wants to send a message, and they're willing to pay top dollar."

Carla looked up from her laptop, her fingers flying over the keys. "I've got the schematics of the warehouse where they're storing the latest shipment. Security's tight, but nothing we can't handle."

Jasmine, adjusting her wig in the mirror, nodded. "I can get us in, no problem. Once we're inside, we'll need to move fast."

Reina, loading her sniper rifle with precision, glanced at Lea. "Who's the client?"

Lea hesitated for a moment before answering. "That's classified. All we need to know is that they have deep pockets and a serious grudge against the Cartel."

The plan was set, and the girls moved with the confidence of seasoned professionals. They knew the risks, but they thrived on the adrenaline and the challenge. Lea led them out into the night, each step bringing them closer to their target.

The warehouse was a fortress, but the Get Money Girls were undeterred. Jasmine's expert infiltration got them past the initial security, and Carla's hacking skills disabled the cameras and alarms. They moved like shadows through the dimly lit corridors, their hearts pounding with anticipation.

As they approached the storage area, Lea signaled for them to stop. "Reina, take point. We need eyes on the guards."

Reina nodded and slipped into position, her sniper scope trained on the warehouse entrance. "Two guards. Armed. Easy targets."

Lea gave the signal, and Reina's shots rang out, silencing the guards before they even knew what hit them. The girls moved in, their steps swift and silent.

Inside, the warehouse was filled with crates of cocaine, the lifeblood of the Cartel's operation. Lea's eyes scanned the room, noting the positions of more guards. They needed to act quickly and decisively.

But just as they began to set their charges, all hell broke loose. An alarm blared, and the warehouse was flooded with armed men. The Get Money Girls had been ambushed.

"Fall back!" Lea shouted, firing her weapon as she retreated. The girls moved with practiced precision, covering each other as they fought their way out. Bullets flew, and the air was thick with the acrid smell of gunpowder.

In the chaos, Reina was hit. Lea's heart clenched as she saw her cousin fall. "Reina! No!"

She rushed to Reina's side, her eyes filled with desperation. Reina's face was pale, her breathing labored. "Go... get out of here," she gasped.

Lea shook her head, tears streaming down her face. "I won't leave you."

But Reina pushed her away, her voice weak but insistent. "You have to... finish the job."

With a final, pained look, Lea nodded. She stood, her resolve hardened by grief and rage. She signaled for the rest of the crew to retreat, covering their escape with a barrage of gunfire. They fought their way out, their hearts heavy with the loss of one of their own.

Back at their headquarters, the mood was somber. The mission had been a disaster, and Reina's death weighed heavily on them all. Lea stood at the window, staring out at the city that had taken so much from her.

"We were set up," Carla said, breaking the silence. "Someone knew we were coming."

Lea nodded, her jaw clenched. "The Cartel. They were ready for us. And now... we have to make them pay."

Jasmine stepped forward, her eyes blazing with determination. "What's the plan, Lea?"

Lea turned to face her crew, her voice steady despite the turmoil inside her. "We find out who set us up. And then we take down the Cartel, piece by piece. No more games."

As they began to plan their next move, Lea couldn't shake the feeling that there was more to this than they realized. She thought about the brief glimpse she had caught of a man during the ambush, a man who had seemed familiar in a way she couldn't explain.

Little did she know, that man was Antonio Lewis, the secret heir of Antonio Brown, and her world was about to collide with his in ways she could never have imagined.

The Get Money Girls were more determined than ever, driven by a thirst for revenge and a need to prove themselves. The streets of Miami were unforgiving, but they were ready to fight back, to reclaim their power and their fallen sister's honor.

Lea's heart burned with a mix of sorrow and anger, her mind filled with thoughts of vengeance. She knew that taking down the Cartel would not be easy, but she was prepared to do whatever it took. The legacy of Antonio Brown had claimed many lives, but it had also brought her face to face with her destiny.

As the Get Money Girls prepared for their next mission, the city of Miami thrummed with anticipation. The battle lines were drawn, and the stage was set for a confrontation that would shake the underworld to its core. Lea and Antonio were on a collision course, their fates intertwined by blood, betrayal, and the relentless pursuit of power.

Chapter 5: A Vow of Vengeance

Lea stood over Reina's grave, the Miami sun beating down on her as she struggled to hold back tears. Her cousin, her sister in arms, was gone, taken by the very world they had vowed to conquer. The funeral had been small and private, attended only by those who truly mattered. As she placed a single white rose on the freshly turned earth, Lea felt a wave of determination wash over her.

"I promise you, Reina," she whispered, her voice trembling with emotion. "I'll make them pay. Every single one of them."

That night, Lea returned to the Get Money Girls' headquarters, her mind consumed by thoughts of vengeance. The loft was quiet, the air heavy with grief and anger. Carla, Jasmine, and the rest of the crew looked to her for guidance, their faces reflecting the same resolve she felt.

"We were set up," Lea began, her voice cold and steady. "The Cartel knew we were coming, and they ambushed us. Reina's death won't be in vain. We're going to take them down, piece by piece."

Carla nodded, her fingers already flying over her laptop. "I'm on it. I'll find their weak spots, the places where we can hit them hardest."

Jasmine, her usual playful demeanor replaced by a steely focus, chimed in. "We need to be smart about this. No more direct hits. We hit them where it hurts the most—money, resources, allies."

Lea nodded, her mind racing with plans and possibilities. "We'll start by gathering intel. Find out everything we can about their operations, their leadership, their vulnerabilities. And then we strike."

As the days turned into weeks, the Get Money Girls threw themselves into their mission. Carla hacked into the Cartel's systems, uncovering a wealth of information about their operations. Jasmine and the others worked the streets, gathering intel from informants and planting seeds of discord among the Cartel's allies.

Lea, meanwhile, became the face of their vengeance. She attended every meeting, led every mission, and inspired her crew with her unwavering determination. She knew that the path ahead was fraught with danger, but she was ready to face it head-on.

One evening, Lea found herself at one of Miami's hottest nightclubs, The Pulse. It was a place where the city's elite and its underworld mingled, a perfect spot for gathering information and making connections. Lea moved through the crowd with ease, her beauty and confidence drawing attention from all sides.

As she made her way to the bar, a handsome man caught her eye. He was tall, with a chiseled jawline and eyes that seemed to see right through her. He flashed her a charming smile, and Lea felt an unexpected flutter in her chest.

"Can I buy you a drink?" he asked, his voice smooth and inviting.

Lea nodded, intrigued. "Sure, why not?"

They chatted for a while, the music pulsing around them as they exchanged flirtatious banter. Lea found herself drawn to him, his charisma and charm a welcome distraction from the darkness that had consumed her life.

"So, what's your name?" she asked, leaning in closer.

"Antonio," he replied, his eyes locking onto hers. "And you?"

"Lea," she said, smiling. "Nice to meet you, Antonio."

Neither of them knew the truth about the other, the secrets they both carried hidden beneath layers of deception. For Lea, Antonio was a brief escape from her mission, a chance to feel something other than anger and grief. For Antonio, Lea was a captivating mystery, a woman who seemed to defy the world around her.

As the night wore on, they found themselves dancing together, their bodies moving in sync with the music. Lea felt a spark of hope, a glimpse of a future that wasn't consumed by violence and revenge. But deep down, she knew that this was only a momentary respite. Her vow of vengeance was still burning bright, and she couldn't afford to lose focus.

When the night finally came to an end, Lea and Antonio exchanged numbers, promising to meet again. Lea couldn't help but feel a sense of excitement, tempered by the knowledge that her true mission was far from over.

Back at the loft, Lea filled her crew in on her night, leaving out the details about Antonio. She couldn't afford any distractions, not now. They continued their work, identifying the Cartel's weak points and planning their next moves.

Days later, Lea received a text from Antonio, inviting her to dinner. She hesitated for a moment before agreeing. She needed to keep her connections strong, and Antonio seemed like someone worth knowing.

The dinner was a whirlwind of laughter and conversation, each of them revealing bits and pieces of their lives while carefully guarding their secrets. Lea felt a growing attraction to Antonio, but she knew she had to stay focused on her mission.

As they walked along the Miami waterfront after dinner, Antonio turned to her, his expression serious. "I feel like there's something you're not telling me, Lea. Something important."

Lea looked away, her mind racing. She couldn't reveal the truth, not yet. "We all have our secrets, Antonio. But I promise, you'll know mine in time."

Antonio nodded, accepting her answer for now. They parted ways, each of them carrying the weight of their hidden lives.

Lea returned to the loft, her resolve stronger than ever. She knew that falling for Antonio could complicate her mission, but she couldn't deny the connection she felt. She had to stay focused, to honor her vow of vengeance for Reina.

The Get Money Girls continued their work, their plans becoming more intricate and their attacks more precise. Lea led them with a fierce determination, knowing that every step brought them closer to their goal.

The streets of Miami were unforgiving, but Lea was ready to face whatever came her way. She would take down the Cartel, piece by piece, and avenge her cousin's death. And maybe, just maybe, she would find a way to let Antonio into her life.

But for now, her focus was on revenge. The Cartel had taken too much from her, and she was determined to make them pay. The path ahead was dark and dangerous, but Lea knew she had the strength to see it through. She would honor Reina's memory and reclaim her power, no matter the cost.

Chapter 6: Love and Lies

Miami's nightlife pulsed with an electric energy, the kind that made promises it couldn't keep. The streets were alive with music and lights, and it was in one of the city's many hotspots that Antonio and Lea's paths crossed again. This time, they were not just strangers sharing a dance, but two people drawn to each other by an inexplicable chemistry that neither could ignore.

Lea arrived at the club with her girls, each of them dressed to kill—literally and figuratively. The Get Money Girls were known for their beauty and their deadly precision, and tonight they were there to unwind. Lea had texted Antonio earlier, suggesting they meet up, and he had readily agreed. She spotted him near the bar, his presence commanding attention despite the crowded room.

"Antonio," she called out over the music, her voice cutting through the noise like a blade.

He turned, a smile spreading across his face as he saw her. "Lea, you look stunning."

They embraced, the physical contact sending a jolt through both of them. As they moved to the dance floor, their bodies seemed to move in perfect sync, each step a testament to the unspoken connection they shared. The night wore on, and their attraction only grew stronger, the air around them thick with unfulfilled promises and unspoken secrets.

Back at Antonio's place later that night, the atmosphere shifted from electric to intimate. The city lights filtered through the windows, casting a soft glow on their faces as they talked, their conversations deep and revealing. But beneath the surface, both Lea and Antonio were hiding their true identities, each wary of what the other might be hiding.

Lea was careful with her words, never letting on about her true mission. She told Antonio about her life in broad strokes, omitting the details of her work as a contract killer and her vow to take down the

Cartel. Antonio, too, was guarded, keeping his connection to the Cartel and his quest to understand his father's empire a secret.

As the weeks passed, their relationship grew more intense. They spent their nights together, their days filled with stolen moments and whispered confessions. The chemistry between them was undeniable, but so was the tension. Both of them were living double lives, and the weight of their secrets threatened to crush them.

Gossip about their relationship began to spread through their respective circles. The Get Money Girls were suspicious of Antonio, wary of the effect he had on Lea. They whispered among themselves, wondering if Lea was losing her edge, if her newfound romance was making her soft.

"Lea, you sure about this guy?" Carla asked one evening as they prepared for a mission. "He seems too good to be true."

Lea shrugged, her eyes focused on her weapon as she cleaned it. "I can handle myself, Carla. Don't worry about me."

But despite her assurances, Lea couldn't shake the feeling that she was walking a dangerous line. Antonio made her feel alive in a way she hadn't felt in years, but she knew that letting her guard down could be deadly.

On the other side of the city, Antonio faced similar scrutiny. The Cartel members were suspicious of his growing attachment to Lea, a woman they knew little about. Isabella, his half-sister, was particularly vocal in her concerns.

"Who is she, Antonio?" Isabella demanded during a family meeting. "You barely know her, and she's already got you wrapped around her finger."

Antonio sighed, rubbing his temples. "I know what I'm doing, Isabella. Lea's different. She's not like the others."

But even as he defended Lea, Antonio felt the strain of their hidden lives. He wanted to trust her, to believe that their connection was real, but he knew that secrets had a way of coming to light in the worst possible ways.

One night, after a particularly heated argument with Isabella, Antonio found himself at Lea's apartment, his mind racing. As they sat on her balcony, looking out over the city, he finally spoke the words that had been haunting him.

"Lea, I need to know something. Are you hiding anything from me?"

Lea's heart skipped a beat, her mind flashing to her mission, to Reina's death, and to the Cartel. She met his gaze, her expression unreadable. "Why do you ask?"

Antonio looked away, struggling to find the right words. "I just feel like there's more to you than what you're telling me. And I know I haven't been completely honest with you either."

Lea took a deep breath, her thoughts racing. She wanted to tell him the truth, to lay everything out in the open, but the stakes were too high. She couldn't afford to let her guard down, not when revenge was so close at hand.

"I think we both have our secrets, Antonio," she said finally, her voice steady. "But maybe that's okay. Maybe we need to take things one step at a time."

Antonio nodded, feeling a mixture of relief and frustration. He wanted to believe her, to trust that they could navigate their secrets together, but he knew that the truth had a way of coming out, no matter how deeply it was buried.

As they sat in silence, the city buzzing around them, both Lea and Antonio wondered how long they could keep their double lives hidden. The chemistry between them was undeniable, but so was the danger. Their love was built on a foundation of lies, and they both knew that it was only a matter of time before everything came crashing down.

In the weeks that followed, the tension within their circles grew. The Get Money Girls continued their mission, their loyalty to Lea unwavering but their suspicions about Antonio growing. The Cartel, meanwhile, watched Antonio closely, wary of his relationship with a woman they didn't trust.

Lea and Antonio's nights were filled with passion and stolen moments, but their days were a constant balancing act. They were drawn to each other, their connection undeniable, but the secrets they kept threatened to destroy everything they had built.

As the stakes grew higher, both Lea and Antonio knew that they would have to make a choice. They could continue to live in the shadows, hiding their true selves from each other, or they could risk everything for a chance at something real.

But in a world as dangerous as theirs, trust was a luxury they couldn't afford. And as they navigated the treacherous waters of love and lies, they both wondered if their secrets would ultimately be their undoing.

Chapter 7: Power Struggles

The sun blazed high in the Miami sky, casting harsh shadows over the sprawling Brown estate. Inside, the atmosphere was equally tense. Antonio sat at the head of the long dining table, surrounded by members of the Cartel, including his half-sisters, Isabella and Sofia. He had been in Miami for weeks now, trying to carve out his place within the empire his father had built. But the road was anything but smooth.

Isabella, the elder of his two half-sisters, was a formidable presence. She had been deeply involved in the Cartel's operations for years and had expected to take over after their father's death. Her resentment towards Antonio was palpable. Sofia, though younger and less experienced, shared her sister's wariness. The two sisters had always been a team, and Antonio's sudden appearance threatened their balance of power.

Antonio cleared his throat, trying to command the room's attention. "We need to tighten our security at the port. The recent hits have shown that our defenses are weak."

Isabella scoffed, leaning back in her chair. "And what makes you an expert on our security, Antonio? You've been here, what, a few weeks? You have no idea how things work around here."

Antonio met her gaze steadily. "I may be new, but I'm not blind. Our father's death has left us vulnerable. We need to adapt, or we risk losing everything."

The room fell silent, the tension thick enough to cut with a knife. Miguel, their father's trusted lieutenant, nodded in agreement. "Antonio's right. We've been hit hard recently. We need to rethink our strategy."

Isabella's eyes flashed with anger. "Fine. But don't think for a second that you're in charge here, Antonio. This is our family, our legacy."

Antonio took a deep breath, fighting to keep his composure. "I'm not trying to take over, Isabella. I just want to help. We're stronger together."

The meeting continued with more heated discussions, but the underlying power struggle was clear. Antonio knew that earning his place within the Cartel would be a battle. The members were divided, some loyal to Isabella and Sofia, others willing to give Antonio a chance. The power vacuum left by his father's death had created a breeding ground for conflict.

After the meeting, Antonio retreated to his father's study, a place that still held the aura of Antonio Brown's dominance. The room was filled with mementos of his father's life, from framed photos to stacks of ledgers detailing the Cartel's operations. Antonio sat at the massive oak desk, feeling the weight of the legacy he was trying to uphold.

Miguel entered, closing the door behind him. "You've got your work cut out for you, Antonio. Isabella and Sofia aren't going to make this easy."

Antonio nodded, his mind racing. "I know. But I have to find a way to earn their trust. The Cartel is on shaky ground, and we can't afford to be divided."

Miguel sighed, sitting across from him. "Your father built this empire through fear and respect. But he also made a lot of enemies. The attacks we've been facing aren't just random. Someone is trying to take us down."

Antonio leaned back in the chair, running a hand through his hair. "I need to understand the full scope of our operations, the alliances, the enemies. My father kept so much from me."

Miguel nodded. "I'll help you. But you have to be ready for the dark realities of this life. Your father wasn't a saint, and neither are the people we deal with."

As Antonio delved deeper into the Cartel's world, he began to uncover the harsh truths that his father had kept hidden. The Cartel's power was built on a foundation of violence, betrayal, and corruption. Every alliance was fragile, every partnership a potential threat. Antonio found himself constantly looking over his shoulder, wary of who he could trust.

The more he learned, the more he understood the complexity of the empire he was now a part of. The Cartel controlled not just the port, but a vast network of operations that extended far beyond Miami. From drug trafficking to money laundering, every aspect of the business was tainted by danger and deceit.

One evening, as he reviewed documents in his father's study, Isabella stormed in, her face flushed with anger. "What do you think you're doing, Antonio? This isn't your place."

Antonio looked up, meeting her fiery gaze. "I'm trying to understand the business, Isabella. If we're going to survive, we need to work together."

Isabella crossed her arms, her voice cold. "You think you can just waltz in here and take over? You have no idea what it takes to run this empire. Father protected you from this world for a reason."

Antonio stood, his frustration boiling over. "I'm not trying to take over. But I'm not going to sit back and watch everything our father built crumble. I want to help."

Isabella's expression softened slightly, but her eyes remained hard. "If you really want to help, you'll need to prove yourself. Actions speak louder than words, Antonio."

In the days that followed, Antonio threw himself into the Cartel's operations, working alongside the enforcers and gaining the respect of some while facing the continued skepticism of others. He dealt with shipments, negotiated deals, and even handled a few skirmishes with rival gangs. Each step was a test, a chance to prove that he was more than just an outsider.

But the internal conflicts persisted. The power struggles within the Cartel grew more intense, with factions forming around different members. Isabella and Sofia had their loyalists, while others began to rally around Antonio, seeing in him a chance for new leadership.

One night, after a particularly brutal confrontation with a rival gang, Antonio found himself alone in his father's study once more. The blood and violence of the day weighed heavily on him, and he felt the enormity of the challenge before him.

As he sat in the dimly lit room, the door creaked open, and Sofia stepped inside. She hesitated before speaking, her voice soft. "Antonio, I know things have been tense. But I want you to know that I don't see you as an enemy. I just... I need to understand why you're here."

Antonio looked at her, seeing the uncertainty in her eyes. "I'm here because this is my family, Sofia. I never knew our father, but I want to honor his legacy. And I want to do it with you and Isabella, not against you."

Sofia nodded slowly, a tentative smile forming on her lips. "Then maybe we can find a way to make this work. Together."

As Sofia left the room, Antonio felt a glimmer of hope. The path ahead was still fraught with challenges, but he knew that with time, he could earn the trust of his family and solidify his place within the Cartel. The power struggles were far from over, but Antonio was ready to fight for his father's empire and carve out his own legacy in the process.

Chapter 8: The Hit Backfires

The night air was thick with tension as Lea and the Get Money Girls gathered in their loft, finalizing plans for their next strike against the Cartel. The ambush that had taken Reina's life still haunted Lea, and she was determined to avenge her cousin's death. Every detail of this mission had been meticulously planned. Carla had hacked into the Cartel's security systems, ensuring they would have an opening. Jasmine had scouted the location for weeks, memorizing every exit and blind spot. Everything was set.

Lea stood before her crew, her expression hard and resolute. "Tonight, we hit them where it hurts. We take out one of their main distribution centers. This is for Reina. Let's do this."

The crew nodded, their faces grim with determination. They moved like shadows through the streets, arriving at the warehouse just as Carla had disabled the security cameras. Lea took a deep breath, signaling her team to move in.

Inside the warehouse, the atmosphere was tense. Stacks of crates filled the space, each one packed with drugs worth millions. Lea and her crew moved quickly, setting charges and taking down the few guards who patrolled the area. Everything was going according to plan—until it wasn't.

A loud alarm suddenly blared, shattering the silence. The warehouse was flooded with light as armed men poured in from every direction. Lea's heart sank. They had been set up.

"Fall back!" she shouted, firing her weapon as she retreated. The Get Money Girls scattered, each of them fighting their way through the ambush. Bullets flew, and the air was filled with the deafening sound of gunfire.

Jasmine was the first to fall, a bullet catching her in the shoulder. Carla and the others fought desperately to cover her, but the Cartel's forces were overwhelming. Lea knew they had to get out, but escape seemed impossible.

They managed to fight their way to an exit, dragging Jasmine with them. The mission was a disaster, and the Cartel had clearly been prepared. Lea's mind raced as they fled into the night, her thoughts filled with anger and confusion. How had they known?

Back at their loft, the mood was somber. Carla worked quickly to tend to Jasmine's wound, but the atmosphere was charged with tension and suspicion. Lea paced the room, her mind replaying the events of the night.

"This doesn't make sense," she muttered, more to herself than anyone else. "They were ready for us. Someone must have tipped them off."

Carla looked up, her face pale and tired. "You think we have a mole?"

Lea stopped pacing, her eyes narrowing. "I don't know. But we need to find out. Someone betrayed us, and we can't move forward until we know who."

The Get Money Girls exchanged uneasy glances. Trust was the foundation of their crew, and the thought of a traitor in their midst was almost too much to bear. But Lea knew they couldn't ignore the possibility.

In the days that followed, Lea and her crew regrouped, tending to their wounds and trying to make sense of the failed mission. Lea's thoughts kept returning to the ambush, replaying every detail in her mind. She began to scrutinize her crew's behavior, looking for any signs of betrayal.

One evening, as the crew gathered to discuss their next steps, Lea addressed them, her voice steady but laced with suspicion. "We need to talk about what happened. Someone tipped off the Cartel, and we need to figure out who."

The room fell silent, the air heavy with tension. Carla spoke up, her voice shaky. "Lea, we're a team. We've always had each other's backs. How can you think one of us would betray the crew?"

Lea's gaze hardened. "I don't want to believe it either, Carla. But we can't ignore the facts. Someone knew about our plans. Someone gave us up."

Jasmine, her arm in a sling, looked around the room, her eyes filled with fear and anger. "We need to find out who did this. We can't move forward until we know we can trust each other."

The crew nodded in agreement, their expressions grim. They began to review their steps leading up to the mission, looking for any signs of a leak. As they combed through their plans and communications, Lea's suspicion grew. Every interaction, every conversation was scrutinized.

Days turned into weeks, and the atmosphere in the loft grew more strained. The once unbreakable bond between the Get Money Girls was fraying, each member wary of the others. Lea felt the weight of leadership pressing down on her, the responsibility of keeping her crew safe while hunting for a traitor.

One night, as Lea sat alone, poring over their plans, she received a text from Antonio. Despite the chaos of her mission, her feelings for him had grown. But the secrets she kept weighed heavily on her heart. She knew that revealing the truth about her mission would jeopardize everything.

"Hey, you okay?" the text read. "I've been thinking about you."

Lea stared at the message, torn between her need for connection and her duty to her crew. She decided to meet him, hoping that being with Antonio might give her some clarity.

They met at a quiet bar, away from the prying eyes of their respective worlds. Antonio sensed her turmoil, his concern evident. "Lea, what's going on? You seem... distracted."

Lea forced a smile, hiding the storm inside her. "Just dealing with some things. It's complicated."

Antonio reached across the table, taking her hand. "You know you can talk to me, right? Whatever it is, we can figure it out."

Lea felt a pang of guilt. She wanted to trust him, to let him in, but the secrets she kept were too dangerous. "I know, Antonio. But some things are just... complicated."

As they sat in silence, Lea's mind raced. She knew that finding the mole within her crew was crucial, but she also knew that her relationship with Antonio was becoming more complicated by the day. The lines between love and lies were blurring, and she feared that the truth would tear everything apart.

Returning to the loft that night, Lea steeled herself. She would find the traitor, and she would avenge Reina's death. The Get Money Girls were more than just a crew—they were her family. And she would protect them, no matter the cost. The Cartel had made a powerful enemy, and Lea was determined to bring them down.

Chapter 9: Uncovering Secrets

Lea's mind raced as she sifted through the intel Carla had gathered. There was something about the way the Cartel had been one step ahead of them that gnawed at her. The failed mission and the ambush seemed too orchestrated. As she combed through the details, a familiar name kept popping up: Antonio Lewis. Her heart skipped a beat. Antonio. The man she had been seeing, the man she was falling for.

Lea's fingers trembled as she clicked through the documents. Antonio's name was linked to the Cartel in ways that were impossible to ignore. It didn't take long for her to piece together the truth—Antonio Lewis was the son of Antonio Brown, the very man whose death had left a power vacuum in the Cartel. Her blood ran cold as the realization sank in. She had been sleeping with the enemy.

That evening, Lea decided she needed answers. She texted Antonio, asking him to meet her at a quiet spot they often visited. Her emotions were a whirlwind of betrayal, anger, and confusion. She had to know the truth.

Antonio arrived at the small, secluded park, his face lighting up when he saw her. "Lea, hey," he greeted, pulling her into an embrace. But Lea remained stiff in his arms.

"Antonio, we need to talk," she said, her voice barely above a whisper.

He pulled back, sensing the tension. "What's wrong?"

Lea took a deep breath, her eyes locking onto his. "Who are you really, Antonio? What's your connection to the Cartel?"

Antonio's expression shifted from confusion to shock, and finally to resignation. He ran a hand through his hair, sighing deeply. "Lea, I didn't want you to find out like this."

"Find out what?" Lea demanded, her voice rising. "That you're Antonio Brown's son? That you're part of the very organization I've been trying to take down?"

Antonio nodded slowly, guilt etched across his face. "Yes, I am his son. But it's not what you think. I didn't know him. I grew up away from all of this. I only came to Miami after his death to understand who he was and what he built."

Lea's eyes filled with tears of frustration. "So you've been lying to me this whole time? Playing me while I was falling for you?"

"No, Lea, it wasn't like that," Antonio insisted, stepping closer. "I had no idea about your mission, about who you were until now. I care about you. That's real."

Lea shook her head, trying to process everything. "Do you have any idea what I've lost because of your family? Reina is dead, Antonio. She died because of the Cartel, and I vowed to bring them down. And now... now I find out you're part of it."

Antonio's face fell, pain and regret evident in his eyes. "I'm so sorry, Lea. I had no idea. If I'd known, I would have told you everything sooner. But you have to believe me—I'm not like my father. I want to change things. I want to make the Cartel something different, something less destructive."

Lea's anger flared. "Less destructive? Do you hear yourself? People are dying, Antonio. Innocent people. And you think you can change that?"

Antonio reached for her hand, his grip firm yet gentle. "I know it sounds impossible, but I have to try. If I walk away now, someone worse will take over, and the cycle of violence will continue. I need your help, Lea. Together, we can make a difference."

Lea stared at him, torn between the man she had come to care for and the mission that had driven her for so long. Could she trust him? Could she put aside her desire for revenge to work with him towards a common goal?

"You want my help?" she asked, her voice trembling. "You think we can take down the Cartel from the inside?"

Antonio nodded, his eyes pleading. "Yes. But we have to be smart. We have to be united. I know it's a lot to ask, but I need you, Lea."

Lea looked away, tears streaming down her face. She thought of Reina, of the life they had dreamed of, free from the violence and chaos of the streets. Could she really align herself with Antonio, the son of the man who had caused so much pain?

After a long silence, Lea turned back to him, her resolve hardening. "I'll help you, Antonio. But know this: if you betray me, if you ever lie to me again, I won't hesitate to take you down."

Antonio nodded solemnly. "I understand. I won't let you down, Lea. We'll do this together."

As they left the park that night, Lea's mind was a storm of conflicting emotions. She knew the path ahead would be fraught with danger and deceit, but for the first time in a long while, she felt a glimmer of hope. Maybe, just maybe, they could find a way to bring down the Cartel and build something better.

The days that followed were a whirlwind of planning and strategy. Lea and Antonio worked together, their connection growing stronger even as they navigated the treacherous waters of their new alliance. They began to identify the Cartel's weak spots, planning their moves with precision and care.

But the secrets they kept from their respective worlds weighed heavily on them. The Get Money Girls were suspicious of Lea's sudden shift in focus, and the Cartel members were wary of Antonio's growing influence. Trust was a rare commodity, and every step they took was a gamble.

One evening, as they sat together in Antonio's apartment, poring over maps and documents, Lea looked up at him, a question burning in her mind. "Antonio, what if this doesn't work? What if we can't change things?"

Antonio met her gaze, his expression serious. "Then we keep fighting, Lea. We keep trying. Because the alternative is unthinkable."

Lea nodded, feeling a surge of determination. They were in this together, for better or worse. And no matter what the future held, they would face it side by side.

As the night wore on, they continued their work, the city of Miami sprawling out beneath them like a battlefield. The stakes were higher than ever, but Lea and Antonio were ready to take on whatever came their way. The Cartel's reign of terror was far from over, but with each step they took, they moved closer to their goal of justice and redemption.

Chapter 10: Allies and Enemies

The stakes had never been higher for both Lea and Antonio. They were playing a dangerous game, one that required them to walk a fine line between their loyalty to their crews and their clandestine alliance. Lea knew she had to rally her girls and prepare them for the impending war, while Antonio had to solidify his power within the Cartel and seek allies who could help him broker peace.

Lea gathered the Get Money Girls in their loft, the atmosphere thick with anticipation. The recent betrayal and the discovery of Antonio's true identity had shaken them, but Lea's leadership was unwavering.

"Listen up," Lea began, her voice firm and steady. "We have a chance to take down the Cartel from the inside. Antonio is on our side, but we need to be ready for anything. This won't be easy, and we can't afford any more mistakes."

Carla, her tech-savvy right hand, nodded. "What's the plan, Lea?"

"We need to identify who we can trust within our own ranks and make sure our operations are airtight," Lea replied. "We also need to gather intel on the Cartel's next moves. They're preparing for war, and we need to be one step ahead."

Jasmine, still recovering from her injuries, spoke up. "And Antonio? Can we really trust him?"

Lea hesitated for a moment before answering. "I believe we can. But we need to keep our eyes open. This is about more than just trust—it's about survival."

As the Get Money Girls strategized and fortified their defenses, Antonio was doing the same within the Cartel. He knew that earning the loyalty of his father's former allies and convincing them to support his vision for a more controlled and less violent operation would be a monumental task.

He met with Miguel, his father's trusted lieutenant, in the dimly lit back room of a high-end Miami nightclub. The tension between them was palpable.

"Miguel, we need to talk," Antonio began, his voice low but resolute. "The Cartel is on the brink of an all-out war. We can't afford to lose control."

Miguel took a sip of his drink, his expression unreadable. "What do you propose, Antonio? Your father's ways kept us in power for years."

Antonio leaned forward, his eyes intense. "I propose we adapt. The world is changing, and we need to change with it. We can't keep operating with the same level of violence and chaos. It's unsustainable."

Miguel studied him for a moment before nodding. "You make a good point. But change won't come easy. There are many who are loyal to the old ways."

"Then we find those who are willing to support a new vision," Antonio insisted. "We broker peace where we can and show strength where we must."

Over the next few days, Antonio and Miguel began to reach out to key figures within the Cartel, gauging their willingness to support a new approach. It was a delicate balancing act, one that required careful negotiation and a display of both power and diplomacy.

Meanwhile, Lea worked tirelessly to secure her own allies. She reached out to former associates and rival crews, forging tentative alliances based on mutual interests and the promise of a common enemy. The streets of Miami buzzed with rumors and speculation, the tension mounting as both sides prepared for the inevitable clash.

One evening, Antonio and Lea met in secret at a secluded beach, the sound of the waves providing a brief respite from the chaos of their lives. They sat on the sand, watching the moonlight dance on the water.

"How's it going on your end?" Lea asked, her voice soft but laced with worry.

Antonio sighed, running a hand through his hair. "It's tough. Some of the old guard are resistant to change, but there are others who see the need for it. We're making progress, but it's slow."

Lea nodded, understanding all too well. "Same here. The girls are on edge, and trust is a fragile thing right now. But we're holding strong."

Antonio turned to her, his expression earnest. "Lea, we have to make this work. If we don't, it's not just us who'll suffer. It's everyone caught in the crossfire."

Lea reached out, taking his hand in hers. "I know. And we will make it work. Together."

Their moment of connection was brief, but it strengthened their resolve. They returned to their respective worlds, more determined than ever to see their plan through.

As the days turned into weeks, the preparations for war intensified. The Get Money Girls tightened their operations, conducting surveillance on Cartel movements and shoring up their defenses. Lea's leadership was crucial, her strategic mind and unyielding determination inspiring her crew to push forward despite the odds.

Antonio, on the other hand, continued to navigate the treacherous waters of Cartel politics. He held meetings with key players, presenting his vision for a more stable and less violent operation. It was a hard sell, but slowly, he began to win over some of the more influential members.

One evening, during a tense meeting with a particularly stubborn lieutenant named Ricardo, Antonio made a bold move. "Ricardo, you've seen what unchecked violence brings. It's bad for business and bad for all of us. Support me, and I promise a more profitable and controlled future."

Ricardo eyed him skeptically before finally nodding. "Alright, Antonio. I'll give you my support. But remember, if you fail, it's your head on the line."

Antonio nodded, relief washing over him. "I won't fail."

Back at the Get Money Girls' loft, Lea received an unexpected visit from an old ally, a former gang leader named Victor. He had heard about their plans and wanted in.

"Lea, I've got a score to settle with the Cartel," Victor said, his voice filled with conviction. "If you're taking them down, I want to help."

Lea smiled, shaking his hand. "Welcome aboard, Victor. We can use all the help we can get."

As the pieces fell into place, both Lea and Antonio knew that the time for action was drawing near. The Cartel and the Get Money Girls were on a collision course, and the outcome would determine the future of Miami's underworld.

The tension in the city was palpable, the air thick with anticipation and fear. Allies were secured, enemies identified, and plans set in motion. Antonio and Lea, each from their own side, worked tirelessly to ensure that when the dust settled, they would be the ones left standing.

The night before the planned confrontation, Antonio and Lea met one last time in secret, their connection a beacon of hope in the dark, chaotic world they inhabited.

"Tomorrow's the day," Antonio said, his voice steady but filled with emotion. "Are you ready?"

Lea nodded, her eyes fierce. "I've never been more ready. Let's end this."

As they parted ways, each returning to their own preparations, they knew that the battle ahead would be fierce and unforgiving. But together, they believed they could change the course of their lives and bring a new era to the streets of Miami. The stage was set for an all-out war, and only time would tell who would emerge victorious.

Chapter 11: The Family Legacy

Antonio sat in his father's study, the room dark except for the dim glow of a desk lamp. The space was filled with relics of Antonio Brown's reign: photos of powerful men, stacks of ledgers, and a safe that held secrets waiting to be uncovered. Antonio knew that understanding his father's legacy was crucial to shaping the future of the Cartel, but the more he learned, the heavier the burden became.

Flipping through a leather-bound journal, Antonio discovered entries detailing deals, betrayals, and bloodshed. His father had been ruthless, his power maintained through fear and violence. Antonio felt a chill run down his spine as he read about the lengths his father had gone to keep control. The morality of the Cartel's operations weighed heavily on him, and he wondered if he was any different from the man whose name he bore.

Late one night, Antonio found an old videotape labeled "Confession." Intrigued, he popped it into an ancient VCR tucked in the corner of the study. The screen flickered to life, revealing his father, older and more haggard than Antonio remembered from the few photos he had seen.

"If you're watching this, I'm probably dead," Antonio Brown began, his voice rough and tired. "This life... it takes everything from you. But it was the only way I knew to protect my family, to give them a future."

Antonio leaned forward, hanging on every word. His father continued, detailing alliances formed and enemies made, admitting to heinous acts committed in the name of power. But there was a moment of vulnerability, a confession of regret.

"I did what I had to do, but I lost myself along the way. If you're my son, Antonio, know that you have a choice. You can be better than I was. You can change things."

Tears welled up in Antonio's eyes as he watched his father's face fade into static. The man he had never known was a complex mix of strength and frailty, power and remorse. Antonio felt a newfound determination to honor his father's wish—to be better.

The next morning, Antonio approached his half-sisters, Isabella and Sofia, who were having breakfast in the grand dining room. The tension between them had lessened over the past weeks, but a lingering wariness remained.

"I need to talk to you both," Antonio said, his voice steady. "I've been learning more about our father's legacy, and I think it's time we face the truth about what he built."

Isabella raised an eyebrow. "And what truth is that?"

"That his empire was built on blood and betrayal," Antonio replied. "But he also wanted something better for us. We have a chance to change things, to make the Cartel something more than just a machine of violence."

Sofia looked thoughtful. "You really believe that? That we can change it?"

"I do," Antonio said firmly. "But we have to do it together. We have to earn the loyalty of our people not through fear, but through respect and strength."

Isabella sighed, putting down her coffee. "You sound like you're actually starting to understand this world. Maybe you're more like our father than I thought."

Antonio met her gaze. "I don't want to be like him. I want to be better. For all of us."

The sisters exchanged glances, a silent agreement passing between them. "Alright, Antonio," Isabella said finally. "We'll give you a chance. But don't think for a second that it's going to be easy."

Antonio nodded, relief washing over him. "I wouldn't expect it to be."

As days turned into weeks, Antonio worked tirelessly to solidify his position within the Cartel. He met with key members, presenting his vision for a more controlled, less violent organization. Slowly but surely, he began to win over those who were tired of the constant bloodshed and instability.

Miguel, his father's lieutenant, became a crucial ally. Together, they worked on strategies to strengthen the Cartel's operations while minimizing collateral damage. Antonio's approach was unconventional, but it began to show results.

Meanwhile, Isabella and Sofia started to see their half-brother in a different light. His dedication and determination were undeniable, and his willingness to face the harsh realities of their world earned him their grudging respect. They began to include him in their plans, recognizing that he brought a fresh perspective that could benefit them all.

One evening, after a particularly grueling meeting, Antonio found himself alone in the study once more. He stared at the portrait of his father that hung above the desk, feeling the weight of his legacy.

"I'm trying, Father," he whispered. "I'm trying to be better, to build something that won't destroy everything it touches."

His thoughts were interrupted by a knock at the door. It was Isabella, her expression softer than usual. "Mind if I come in?"

"Of course not," Antonio replied, gesturing to a chair.

She sat down, looking around the room before her eyes settled on him. "You've been doing good work, Antonio. I didn't think I'd ever say this, but I'm starting to believe in your vision."

Antonio smiled, a sense of accomplishment warming his heart. "Thank you, Isabella. That means a lot."

"But don't get too comfortable," she added with a smirk. "We still have a long way to go."

"I know," Antonio said. "And I'm ready for whatever comes next."

As they continued to talk, Antonio felt a growing sense of unity within his fractured family. The power struggles were far from over, but there was a newfound sense of purpose and direction. Antonio's journey to uncover his father's secrets had brought him closer to the man he had never known, and it had given him the strength to forge his own path.

The Cartel was changing, slowly but surely. Antonio's vision of a more controlled and respected organization was taking shape, and his half-sisters were beginning to see the value in his approach. The road ahead was still fraught with challenges, but for the first time, Antonio felt that they were on the right path.

As he looked out over the Miami skyline, Antonio knew that his father's legacy was a heavy burden, but it was also a source of strength. He was determined to honor the good in his father's intentions and to build something that would stand the test of time. The Cartel would be a force to be reckoned with, but it would also be something more—a family bound by loyalty, respect, and a shared vision for a better future.

Chapter 12: Betrayal from Within

The tension in the air was palpable as Lea paced the loft, her mind racing with the realization that there was a mole within the Get Money Girls. The failed hit against the Cartel had been too perfectly timed, and someone had tipped them off. Her crew watched her nervously, aware that the next steps would be critical.

Lea stopped abruptly and faced her team, her eyes blazing with determination. "We've been betrayed," she said, her voice steady but cold. "Someone here has been feeding information to the Cartel. We need to find out who."

Carla, her tech-savvy right hand, frowned. "Lea, you know we're loyal. None of us would do that."

Lea's gaze softened slightly, but her resolve remained firm. "I want to believe that, Carla. But we can't ignore the facts. I need everyone to be honest. If you know anything, now's the time to speak up."

The room was silent, the weight of suspicion hanging heavy. Lea scanned their faces, looking for any sign of guilt. Her eyes settled on Jasmine, who had been unusually quiet since the ambush. Lea's heart sank at the thought, but she knew she had to be thorough.

"Jasmine," Lea said, her voice gentle but firm. "Is there something you want to tell us?"

Jasmine looked up, her eyes filled with tears. "Lea, I swear I didn't betray you. I've been with you through everything. Why would I turn on you now?"

Lea's heart ached at the sight of Jasmine's pain, but she had to be sure. "Then who did, Jasmine? Someone did, and we need to find out who."

As they continued to question each other, the tension grew. Lea could feel the unity of her crew fraying at the edges. Suddenly, Carla's phone buzzed, and she glanced at the screen, her face paling.

"Lea," Carla said urgently, "I just got an alert. There's movement near our stash house. It's the Cartel."

Lea's eyes narrowed. "They're making a move. We need to get there, now."

The Get Money Girls armed themselves quickly, their movements precise and practiced. They raced through the streets of Miami, their destination clear. As they approached the stash house, Lea's suspicions grew. How had the Cartel known about this location? The answer became chillingly clear as they burst through the doors.

Inside, the stash house was a scene of chaos. Cartel enforcers were already there, tearing through their supplies. Lea's heart pounded as she realized the extent of the betrayal. Her crew spread out, engaging in a fierce firefight with the intruders. Bullets flew, and the air was thick with the acrid smell of gunpowder.

Lea spotted a familiar figure in the midst of the chaos. It was Tony, one of her newer recruits, who had always seemed eager to prove himself. Her blood ran cold as she saw him directing the Cartel enforcers, his betrayal clear.

"Tony!" Lea shouted, her voice cutting through the noise. "How could you?"

Tony turned, his face twisted with fear and regret. "Lea, I didn't want this. They made me do it. They threatened my family."

Lea's heart ached with a mix of anger and pity. "You should have come to me, Tony. We could have protected you."

Before he could respond, a bullet struck him in the chest, and he fell to the ground, lifeless. Lea felt a surge of rage and sadness, but there was no time to mourn. The battle raged on, and she fought with a fury born of betrayal.

As the shootout reached its climax, the Cartel enforcers began to retreat, their numbers dwindling. Lea's crew was battered but victorious. The cost, however, was high. Several of her girls were wounded, and the trust that had once bound them together was shattered.

Back at the loft, the atmosphere was somber. Lea tended to Jasmine's wounds, her mind heavy with the weight of what had transpired. The betrayal had cut deep, and the consequences were far-reaching.

Just as Lea began to process the day's events, her phone buzzed. It was Antonio. She answered, her voice tired. "Antonio, now's not a good time."

"Lea, I heard about the shootout," Antonio said, his voice filled with concern. "Are you okay?"

Lea sighed, her exhaustion palpable. "We're alive, but we took a hit. We had a mole. One of my own."

"I'm so sorry," Antonio said, his heart aching for her. "I wish there was something I could do."

"Just be careful, Antonio," Lea replied. "This war is far from over."

Their conversation was cut short by a loud knock on the loft door. Lea's crew tensed, their hands reaching for their weapons. Lea motioned for them to stay back as she approached the door, her heart pounding. She opened it cautiously, her eyes widening in shock.

Standing in the doorway was Isabella, Antonio's half-sister, flanked by two Cartel enforcers. Lea's mind raced, wondering what could have brought her here.

"Isabella," Lea said, her voice cold. "What do you want?"

Isabella's expression was unreadable. "We need to talk. This war is spiraling out of control, and we need to find a way to end it before more blood is shed."

Lea's eyes narrowed. "And why should I trust you?"

Isabella took a deep breath. "Because despite our differences, we both want the same thing—to stop the violence and protect our families. We can't do that if we're constantly at each other's throats."

Lea considered her words carefully. She knew that Isabella was as ruthless as her father, but there was a glimmer of truth in her eyes. Reluctantly, she stepped aside, allowing Isabella to enter.

Inside, the tension was thick as Isabella and Lea faced each other, the weight of their respective worlds pressing down on them. Antonio's relationship with Lea had already strained his ties with the Cartel, and this unexpected meeting only added to the complexity.

"Talk," Lea said, crossing her arms. "What's your plan?"

Isabella glanced around the room, noting the wary expressions of the Get Money Girls. "We need to find common ground. Antonio has been trying to bring some order to the Cartel, and I believe we can work together to find a solution. But we need to build trust."

Lea's eyes flashed with anger. "Trust? After everything that's happened? After Tony's betrayal?"

Isabella nodded, her expression somber. "I know it's a lot to ask. But if we don't try, this war will destroy us all."

Lea felt a wave of exhaustion wash over her. The battle, the betrayal, and the constant strain of leadership had taken their toll. She knew that Isabella was right. They couldn't continue on this path without tearing each other apart.

"Fine," Lea said finally. "We'll talk. But if you cross me, Isabella, I won't hesitate to take you down."

Isabella nodded, a hint of respect in her eyes. "Understood."

As the night wore on, the loft became a place of uneasy truce. The Get Money Girls watched warily as Isabella outlined her proposal for peace, her words echoing Antonio's vision of a less violent, more controlled operation.

Lea listened, her heart torn between her desire for revenge and her hope for a better future. The path ahead was fraught with danger and uncertainty, but for the first time, there was a glimmer of possibility.

As dawn broke over Miami, Lea and Isabella shook hands, their alliance tenuous but real. The war was far from over, but there was a chance—just a chance—that they could find a way to end the bloodshed and build something new. Together.

Chapter 13: The Long Arm of the Law

Antonio stood on the balcony of his father's mansion, overlooking the sprawling city of Miami. The morning air was thick with tension, the calm before the storm. He knew the authorities were closing in, their crackdown on the Cartel intensifying with each passing day. The once seemingly untouchable empire his father had built was now teetering on the brink of collapse.

Inside, the mansion was abuzz with activity. Members of the Cartel moved frantically, shredding documents, destroying evidence, and making desperate phone calls. Antonio's half-sisters, Isabella and Sofia, were in the living room, discussing their next move with Miguel and a few other key lieutenants. The atmosphere was one of barely contained panic.

"We need to get out of here," Isabella said, her voice strained. "The feds are closing in, and it's only a matter of time before they raid this place."

Miguel nodded, his usually calm demeanor replaced by a look of grim determination. "We've already lost several key members. We can't afford to lose anyone else."

Antonio walked into the room, his presence commanding attention. "We're not running," he said firmly. "If we scatter, we lose everything. We need to stay together and figure out how to ride this out."

Sofia looked at him, her eyes wide with fear. "But how, Antonio? They've already arrested Raul and Victor. Who's next?"

Antonio took a deep breath, his mind racing. "We need to be smart. We have to anticipate their moves and stay one step ahead. And we need to make sure our people know that we're still in control."

Just as he finished speaking, the sound of sirens filled the air. Everyone in the room froze, their eyes darting to the windows. The panic was palpable.

"Go!" Antonio shouted. "Everyone, get to the safe house. Now!"

The Cartel members scrambled, grabbing what they could and rushing out of the mansion. Antonio stayed behind for a moment, making sure Isabella and Sofia were safely on their way. He knew that as the leader, he had to be the last to leave.

As he made his way to his car, Antonio's phone buzzed. It was Lea. He answered quickly, his voice tense. "Lea, what is it?"

"Antonio, I just heard. They're raiding your place. Are you okay?" Lea's voice was filled with concern.

"I'm fine," Antonio replied, starting the engine. "But things are bad. We're heading to the safe house."

"Be careful," Lea said. "I'll meet you there."

Antonio hung up and sped away from the mansion, his mind racing with thoughts of their next move. The authorities were tightening the noose, and he knew they had to act fast to avoid complete destruction.

At the safe house, the atmosphere was equally tense. Cartel members huddled together, exchanging worried glances. Antonio stood at the center, trying to project an air of calm authority despite the chaos.

"We need to lay low for a while," he said, addressing the group. "No unnecessary contact, no risky moves. We stick to our plan and wait for this to blow over."

Miguel approached him, his expression serious. "Antonio, we need to talk. The feds have a list of names, and yours is on it. They're coming for you."

Antonio's heart sank. He knew this day would come, but the reality was still a punch to the gut. "We'll deal with it," he said, trying to sound more confident than he felt. "For now, we need to focus on keeping the Cartel together."

As the hours passed, Antonio worked tirelessly to coordinate with his remaining allies, ensuring that operations continued as smoothly as possible despite the mounting pressure. He knew that the Cartel's survival depended on their ability to adapt and stay united.

Meanwhile, Lea was doing her part to support Antonio. She reached out to her contacts, gathering information on the law enforcement's next moves and relaying it back to Antonio. The two of them worked as a seamless team, their bond growing stronger with each challenge they faced.

Late one night, as Antonio was poring over documents in the safe house, Lea arrived, her face etched with worry. "Antonio, we need to talk."

He looked up, his exhaustion evident. "What's going on, Lea?"

She sat down beside him, her expression serious. "I've been hearing things. The feds are planning a major operation. They're not just going after the Cartel—they're coming for you specifically. You need to be ready."

Antonio nodded, his mind racing. "I've been expecting this. But I can't leave. If I run, the Cartel falls apart."

Lea took his hand, her eyes filled with determination. "Then we fight. We find a way to protect you and the Cartel. But you need to promise me that you'll be careful. I can't lose you, Antonio."

He squeezed her hand, feeling a surge of resolve. "I promise, Lea. We'll get through this. Together."

In the days that followed, the Cartel braced for the inevitable confrontation with law enforcement. Antonio tightened security, moved operations to more secure locations, and worked closely with his trusted lieutenants to ensure that their plans were airtight.

Despite the looming threat, there were moments of hope. Antonio's half-sisters, who had initially been skeptical of his leadership, began to see him in a new light. They saw his dedication, his willingness to fight for their family, and his determination to honor their father's legacy while making it his own.

One evening, as the sun set over the Miami skyline, Isabella approached Antonio. "You're doing a good job, you know," she said, her tone softer than usual.

Antonio looked at her, surprised. "Thank you, Isabella. That means a lot."

She nodded, a small smile playing on her lips. "We still have a long way to go, but I believe in what you're trying to do. I just wanted you to know that."

Antonio felt a sense of pride and relief. "I appreciate that. We need to stick together if we're going to make it through this."

As the crackdown continued, Antonio and his allies worked tirelessly to stay one step ahead. They moved quickly, anticipating raids and avoiding capture. But the pressure was relentless, and Antonio knew that it was only a matter of time before the feds closed in on him.

The night finally came when Antonio's worst fears were realized. A team of federal agents stormed the safe house, their shouts and the sound of gunfire filling the air. Antonio fought desperately to protect his people, but he knew that the walls were closing in.

As he faced the agents, his mind flashed to Lea, to his half-sisters, and to the legacy he had fought so hard to protect. He felt a surge of determination. This wasn't the end. He would find a way to keep fighting, to keep the Cartel together.

In the chaos, Antonio was taken into custody, his hands cuffed behind his back. As he was led away, he locked eyes with Miguel, who gave him a nod of encouragement. This was just another battle in a long war, and Antonio was far from done.

As the agents drove him away, Antonio felt a sense of resolve. He would find a way to survive this, to protect his family and his legacy. The Cartel's fight was far from over, and he was determined to see it through to the end.

Chapter 14: Love in the Crossfire

The Miami night was heavy with tension as Antonio and Lea found themselves holed up in a dilapidated safe house on the outskirts of the city. The crackdown on the Cartel had intensified, and the authorities were closing in fast. Antonio could feel the weight of the world on his shoulders as he paced the room, his thoughts a whirlwind of strategy and survival. Lea watched him, her own mind racing with fears and doubts.

"We can't keep running like this, Antonio," Lea said, her voice breaking the silence. "We're running out of places to hide, and the walls are closing in on us."

Antonio stopped pacing and looked at her, his eyes filled with a mix of determination and despair. "I know, Lea. But we have to keep fighting. We can't let them win."

Lea stood up and walked over to him, her expression fierce. "I'm not talking about giving up, Antonio. I'm talking about finding a way to survive this. Together."

Antonio took her hands in his, feeling the warmth and strength she brought him. "We will, Lea. But we need to be smart. We need to stay one step ahead."

Just as they were about to discuss their next move, the sound of sirens echoed in the distance. Antonio's heart raced as he realized they had been found. "They're here," he whispered, his grip tightening on Lea's hands. "We need to go. Now."

They grabbed their bags and bolted for the back door, their footsteps echoing in the narrow alleyways as they ran. The sirens grew louder, and they could hear the shouts of law enforcement and the thudding of boots on the pavement. Lea's heart pounded in her chest as she glanced back, seeing the flashing lights closing in.

"We need to split up," Antonio said breathlessly as they reached a fork in the alley. "We'll have a better chance if we divide their forces."

Lea shook her head, panic in her eyes. "No, Antonio. We stay together. We're stronger that way."

Antonio hesitated for a moment, then nodded. "Alright. Let's keep moving."

They darted through the maze of alleyways, their breaths coming in ragged gasps as they pushed themselves to the limit. The city seemed to close in around them, every corner bringing a new obstacle, a new threat. They could hear the barking of dogs, the shouts of officers, and the ominous hum of helicopters overhead.

As they turned a corner, they found themselves face-to-face with a group of Cartel enforcers. Lea's blood ran cold as she recognized them—these were men she had fought before, men who would not hesitate to kill them on sight.

"Antonio Lewis," one of the enforcers sneered, raising his weapon. "Your time's up."

Antonio pulled Lea behind him, his eyes blazing with defiance. "If you want to take me down, you'll have to go through us."

A tense standoff ensued, the air thick with the threat of violence. The enforcers hesitated, knowing that any move could trigger a deadly shootout. Lea's mind raced as she calculated their options, trying to find a way out.

Suddenly, the sound of gunfire erupted from behind the enforcers. They turned in confusion, giving Antonio and Lea the moment they needed. They sprinted past the distracted men, their hearts pounding as they continued their desperate escape.

They finally reached an abandoned warehouse, ducking inside to catch their breath. Antonio leaned against the wall, his chest heaving. "We can't keep doing this, Lea. We need a plan."

Lea nodded, her eyes wide with fear and determination. "We need to get out of the city. Lay low until things cool down."

Antonio looked at her, his face filled with anguish. "But what about our crews? What about everything we've built?"

Lea stepped closer, placing a hand on his cheek. "Our crews can take care of themselves. Right now, we need to take care of each other."

Their eyes locked, the intensity of their connection filling the space between them. For a moment, the chaos of the world outside faded away, leaving only the two of them. They kissed, a desperate, passionate embrace that spoke of their love and their fear.

But the moment was fleeting. The sound of approaching footsteps brought them back to reality. "We need to move," Antonio said, breaking away reluctantly.

They made their way through the warehouse, finding an old service entrance that led to a hidden alley. As they stepped out into the cool night air, they knew they were running out of options. Every move they made seemed to bring them closer to capture, closer to the end of their fight.

"We have to find a way out of the city," Lea said, her voice filled with determination. "There's a safe house in the Keys. It's off the grid, and we can hide there."

Antonio nodded, his mind racing with the logistics of their escape. "Alright. Let's go."

As they made their way to a stolen car parked nearby, Antonio felt a surge of hope. They could make it. They could survive this. But as they drove through the darkened streets of Miami, he couldn't shake the feeling that their time was running out.

Their journey was fraught with tension, every checkpoint and roadblock a potential trap. They moved carefully, avoiding the main roads and sticking to the shadows. The miles stretched on, the silence between them filled with unspoken fears and doubts.

As dawn began to break, they finally reached the outskirts of the city. The road ahead seemed to stretch endlessly, a path to an uncertain future. Antonio glanced at Lea, her face etched with exhaustion and resolve.

"We're almost there," he said, his voice a mix of reassurance and desperation.

Lea nodded, her eyes fixed on the horizon. "We can do this, Antonio. We have to."

But even as they drove on, Antonio knew that their journey was far from over. The forces that pursued them were relentless, and the challenges they faced would only grow more intense. Their love had brought them this far, but the crossfire of their worlds threatened to tear them apart.

As they crossed the city limits, the weight of their choices settled heavily on their shoulders. They had fought for their love, for their survival, but the cost was high. The road ahead was uncertain, filled with danger and sacrifice. But together, they would face whatever came next, determined to find a way to live, to love, and to survive in the chaotic world they inhabited.

Chapter 15: The Ultimate Betrayal

The atmosphere in the Cartel's safe house was heavy with tension. Antonio had been on edge ever since their escape from the city, his mind racing with the knowledge that a mole was still embedded deep within their ranks. The crackdown from law enforcement had only intensified, and every day brought new challenges and threats. Trust was a rare commodity, and betrayal lurked around every corner.

Antonio sat in the dimly lit room, a map of Miami spread out before him. His mind was preoccupied with strategies to protect his family and his empire, but a nagging suspicion gnawed at him. Someone within the Cartel was orchestrating their downfall from the inside.

Meanwhile, Lea was on her own mission. She had been determined to find out who had hired her to take down the Cartel, suspecting that there was more to the story than she had initially realized. Her contacts had finally come through, and she was about to uncover the truth.

Lea met with Carla in a secluded parking garage, the shadows providing a cloak of secrecy. "You got the info?" Lea asked, her voice a mix of anticipation and dread.

Carla nodded, handing her a thick envelope. "Everything's in there. But Lea, you need to be careful. This goes deeper than we thought."

Lea opened the envelope, her eyes scanning the documents inside. As she read, her heart sank. The person who had hired her to take down the Cartel was none other than Miguel, Antonio's trusted lieutenant. The realization hit her like a punch to the gut. She had been played, manipulated into a deadly game of power and betrayal.

Her mind raced as she tried to process the implications. Miguel had used her to destabilize the Cartel, to create chaos from within. And Antonio had no idea. Lea knew she had to act quickly. She needed to warn Antonio before it was too late.

Back at the safe house, Antonio was discussing their next move with his half-sisters, Isabella and Sofia, when Lea burst into the room, her face pale and eyes wide with urgency.

"Antonio, we need to talk. Now," she said, her voice trembling with intensity.

Antonio looked up, concern etched across his face. "What is it, Lea?"

Lea took a deep breath, holding up the envelope. "I found out who hired me to take down the Cartel. It was Miguel. He's been playing us all."

The room fell silent as Antonio processed the revelation. His mind flashed back to the moments of doubt, the times when Miguel's actions had seemed suspect but he had dismissed them. Rage and betrayal surged through him.

"Miguel," he growled, his fists clenching. "He's been behind this the whole time."

Isabella and Sofia exchanged shocked glances. "Antonio, what are we going to do?" Sofia asked, her voice shaking.

"We confront him," Antonio said, his voice steely with resolve. "And we end this."

Lea nodded, her expression hardening. "I'm with you. We take him down together."

They moved quickly, gathering their most trusted allies and arming themselves for the confrontation. The tension was palpable as they made their way to the location where Miguel was hiding out, a luxurious penthouse on the outskirts of the city.

Antonio led the way, his mind focused on the task at hand. They burst into the penthouse, catching Miguel off guard. He stood in the middle of the room, flanked by a few loyal enforcers, his face a mask of surprise and defiance.

"Antonio," Miguel said, his voice dripping with false bravado. "What's the meaning of this?"

Antonio stepped forward, his eyes blazing with fury. "You know damn well what this is about. You betrayed us, Miguel. You hired Lea to take us down from the inside."

Miguel's face twisted into a sneer. "And what if I did? The Cartel needed new leadership, someone with the vision and strength to take it to the next level."

Antonio's grip tightened on his weapon. "You thought you could play us, use us for your own gain. But it ends here."

The tension in the room reached a boiling point as Antonio and Miguel faced off. The enforcers on both sides raised their weapons, ready for the inevitable clash.

"Last chance, Miguel," Antonio said, his voice low and dangerous. "Surrender, and maybe we'll let you live."

Miguel laughed, a cold, mirthless sound. "You don't have the guts, Antonio. You're just a kid playing at being a leader."

With a roar of fury, Antonio lunged forward. The room erupted into chaos as gunfire rang out, the air thick with smoke and the acrid smell of gunpowder. Lea fought alongside Antonio, her movements swift and deadly, her mind focused on one goal: taking down Miguel.

In the midst of the chaos, Antonio and Miguel grappled, their fight a brutal clash of strength and will. Miguel was strong, but Antonio's rage fueled his every move. He landed a series of punishing blows, his fists connecting with Miguel's face and body.

Miguel staggered back, blood streaming from a cut above his eye. "You can't stop this, Antonio," he spat. "The Cartel is mine."

"Not anymore," Antonio growled, his voice filled with determination. With one final, powerful strike, he sent Miguel crashing to the floor. The room fell silent as Antonio stood over him, breathing heavily, his face a mask of triumph and fury.

Miguel looked up at him, a flicker of fear in his eyes. "You think you've won? This is far from over."

Antonio aimed his weapon at Miguel, his hand steady. "It's over for you, Miguel."

With a final, decisive pull of the trigger, Antonio ended the threat that had been lurking within the Cartel. The enforcers who had sided with Miguel dropped their weapons, surrendering to Antonio's authority.

Lea moved to Antonio's side, her eyes meeting his. "You did it," she said softly. "You stopped him."

Antonio nodded, his expression hard. "But at what cost, Lea? This isn't the end. It's just the beginning of a new fight."

As they secured the penthouse and dealt with the aftermath, Antonio couldn't shake the feeling of betrayal that lingered in his heart. Miguel had been someone he had trusted, someone who had been a part of his father's legacy. And now, that legacy was tainted by deceit and treachery.

Lea stood beside him, her hand resting on his arm. "We'll get through this, Antonio. Together."

Antonio looked at her, his eyes filled with a mix of gratitude and determination. "I know, Lea. We have to. For the Cartel, and for us."

As the night wore on, the reality of their situation set in. They had won a battle, but the war was far from over. The Cartel needed to be rebuilt, trust needed to be restored, and new threats would undoubtedly emerge.

But for now, Antonio and Lea stood together, their bond stronger than ever. They had faced betrayal, fought side by side, and emerged victorious. The road ahead was uncertain, but they were ready to face it together, determined to forge a new path for the Cartel and for themselves.

Chapter 16: The Final Stand

The atmosphere in the Cartel's safe house was electric with tension. The news of Miguel's betrayal had spread like wildfire, and the stakes had never been higher. Antonio stood at the center of the room, surrounded by his most trusted lieutenants and his half-sisters, Isabella and Sofia. They were preparing for what would undoubtedly be the final, decisive battle against The Get Money Girls.

"We can't afford any more mistakes," Antonio said, his voice firm and resolute. "This ends tonight. We either take them down, or we lose everything."

Isabella nodded, her expression steely. "We're with you, Antonio. We've come too far to back down now."

Sofia added, "We need to hit them hard and fast. Show them that we're not going to be taken down easily."

Meanwhile, across town, Lea gathered her crew. The loss of her cousin and the revelation of Miguel's manipulations had galvanized them. They were ready to end this once and for all.

"We've been through hell and back," Lea said, her voice strong and unwavering. "But tonight, we fight for our future. We take the Cartel down, and we make them pay for everything they've done."

Carla, her loyal second-in-command, stepped forward. "What's the plan, Lea?"

Lea outlined their strategy, knowing that this would be their most dangerous mission yet. They would attack the Cartel's main stronghold, catching them off guard and dealing a decisive blow.

As night fell, both sides prepared for the confrontation. The streets of Miami buzzed with anticipation, the air thick with the promise of violence. Antonio and Lea exchanged a brief, intense phone call, each knowing that their love would be tested to the limit.

"Be careful," Antonio said, his voice filled with emotion.

"You too," Lea replied, her heart heavy. "I'll see you on the other side."

The Cartel fortified their position, their enforcers armed to the teeth and ready for battle. Antonio stood at the front, his mind focused on the task at hand. He knew that this was a fight for survival, not just for himself but for everyone who depended on him.

The Get Money Girls moved silently through the city, their steps purposeful and their resolve unshakable. Lea led them, her mind sharp and her heart steeled for the coming fight. She knew that they had to strike hard and fast, taking the Cartel by surprise.

As they approached the Cartel's stronghold, the tension reached a fever pitch. The first shots rang out, shattering the silence and signaling the start of the battle. Bullets flew, and the air was filled with the deafening sounds of gunfire and explosions.

Antonio directed his men with precision, their movements coordinated and deadly. He fought with a fierce determination, knowing that everything was on the line. Isabella and Sofia were by his side, their own skills honed by years of living in the shadow of their father's empire.

Lea and her crew advanced, their attacks swift and brutal. They moved through the stronghold like a storm, leaving chaos and destruction in their wake. Lea's heart pounded as she fought, her mind focused on taking down the Cartel's defenses.

In the midst of the chaos, Antonio and Lea found themselves face-to-face. Their eyes met, and for a brief moment, the world around them seemed to fade away. They were caught between their loyalty to their crews and their love for each other, torn between duty and desire.

"Lea," Antonio said, his voice strained. "We don't have to do this. We can find another way."

Lea shook her head, tears streaming down her face. "It's too late, Antonio. This is the only way."

Their moment was shattered by the sound of an explosion, and they were forced to separate, each returning to their respective battles. The fight raged on, with significant casualties on both sides. Friends and allies fell, their losses a stark reminder of the cost of their struggle.

Antonio fought his way through the stronghold, his every move calculated and lethal. He knew that he had to find Lea, to end this once and for all. As he advanced, he saw his men falling, their blood staining the ground. The weight of their sacrifices fueled his resolve.

Lea pushed forward, her eyes scanning the chaos for any sign of Antonio. She knew that their love would not save them tonight, that only their strength and determination could see them through. She fought with a ferocity born of desperation, her every move a testament to her skill and will.

The battle reached its climax as Antonio and Lea found themselves facing each other once more, their weapons raised and their hearts heavy with the weight of their choices. They stood in the wreckage of their worlds, the echoes of their pasts haunting their every breath.

"Lea," Antonio said, his voice breaking. "I love you. But I can't let you take everything we've built."

Lea's eyes were filled with pain and determination. "I love you too, Antonio. But this is bigger than us. We have to do what's right."

With a final, heartbreaking resolve, they lunged at each other, their weapons clashing in a deadly dance. The world around them blurred as they fought, their love and loyalty colliding in a storm of violence and passion.

As the dust settled and the smoke cleared, Antonio and Lea stood panting, their bodies bruised and bloodied. The stronghold was in ruins, and the losses on both sides were staggering. But amidst the devastation, there was a sense of finality.

Antonio dropped his weapon, his eyes locked on Lea's. "It's over," he said, his voice heavy with sorrow.

Lea nodded, tears streaming down her face. "Yes, it is."

They stood together in the aftermath, their love and their loyalty forever changed by the battle they had fought. The Cartel and The Get Money Girls had been brought to their knees, but Antonio and Lea had survived.

As they walked away from the wreckage, hand in hand, they knew that the road ahead would be filled with challenges. But they also knew that they had each other, and that together, they could face whatever the future held. Their love had been tested in the fires of war, and it had emerged stronger than ever.

Chapter 17: Aftermath

The sun rose over Miami, casting a grim light on the aftermath of the epic confrontation between the Cartel and The Get Money Girls. The stronghold, once a symbol of Antonio Brown's iron-fisted rule, now lay in ruins, a testament to the fierce battle that had unfolded the night before. The streets were eerily quiet, the usual hustle and bustle replaced by an uneasy calm. The community was in shock, reeling from the violent clash that had left a permanent mark on their neighborhood.

Antonio stood on the balcony of what remained of the stronghold, looking out over the city. The cost of the battle was heavy on his mind, the weight of the lives lost and the destruction wrought pressing down on him. His half-sisters, Isabella and Sofia, were inside, tending to the wounded and trying to restore some semblance of order. Antonio knew that the power structure within the Cartel had shifted dramatically, and it was up to him to rebuild it from the ashes.

Lea approached him quietly, her presence a comforting balm to his troubled thoughts. Her face was etched with grief and exhaustion, but there was a steely determination in her eyes. She had lost many of her crew in the fight, and the pain of those losses was a heavy burden.

"Antonio," she said softly, placing a hand on his arm. "We need to talk."

He turned to her, his eyes reflecting the same sorrow and resolve. "I know, Lea. There's so much to deal with."

They moved inside, finding a quiet corner away from the chaos. Antonio's office, once a hub of Cartel operations, was now a makeshift war room. Maps, plans, and weapons lay scattered across the desk, remnants of their desperate fight for survival.

"We've lost a lot," Lea began, her voice steady but filled with emotion. "Both of us. But we're still here. We need to figure out what comes next."

Antonio nodded, running a hand through his hair. "The Cartel is in shambles. We need to reestablish control, regain the trust of our people. And we need to make sure something like this never happens again."

Lea sighed, her eyes reflecting the weight of their shared burdens. "We also need to think about the community. They're scared, confused. They need to see that we're not just about violence and power. We need to show them that we can bring stability."

As they spoke, the news of the battle and its aftermath spread through the neighborhood. The community was abuzz with gossip and speculation, the details of the clash becoming more sensational with each retelling. People gathered in small groups, discussing the events in hushed tones, their eyes darting nervously.

Marta, an elderly woman who had lived in the neighborhood for decades, shook her head as she spoke to a group of neighbors. "These young ones, always fighting. They don't understand what it does to the rest of us. We just want peace."

Her sentiment was echoed by many, the desire for stability and safety overshadowing the fear and uncertainty that had gripped the community. The violent clash had left them wary, but there was also a glimmer of hope that things might change for the better.

Back at the stronghold, Antonio and Lea continued to strategize. They knew that rebuilding the Cartel wouldn't be easy, but they were determined to create a more sustainable and less violent organization. Antonio's half-sisters joined them, their support crucial in rallying the remaining loyalists.

Isabella, her face bruised but her spirit unbroken, spoke up. "We need to reach out to our allies, assure them that we're still in control. We also need to be honest about what happened. Transparency will help rebuild trust."

Sofia nodded in agreement. "And we need to take care of our people. Show them that we value their loyalty, that we're willing to protect and support them."

Antonio looked at his sisters, pride swelling in his chest. "You're right. We start by addressing our crew. We acknowledge our losses, but we also focus on the future."

That evening, Antonio and Lea stood before the assembled members of the Cartel. The mood was somber, the faces of the gathered men and women reflecting the pain and uncertainty of the past days. Antonio took a deep breath, his heart heavy with the responsibility of leadership.

"We've been through hell," he began, his voice strong and clear. "We've lost friends, family. But we're still here. And as long as we stand together, we can rebuild. We can make something better out of this."

Lea stepped forward, her gaze sweeping over the crowd. "We need to learn from our mistakes, to be stronger and smarter. We need to protect each other, to be a family in the truest sense of the word."

The crowd murmured in agreement, the sense of unity and determination palpable. Antonio continued, "We will honor the memories of those we've lost by building a Cartel that they would be proud of. One that stands for strength, but also for community and loyalty."

The days that followed were filled with hard work and careful planning. Antonio, Lea, Isabella, and Sofia worked tirelessly to restore order and stability. They reached out to allies, brokered new deals, and ensured that their operations ran smoothly. The community began to see the changes, the shift towards a more controlled and respectful organization.

One afternoon, as Antonio and Lea walked through the neighborhood, they were approached by Marta. She looked up at them, her eyes filled with a mixture of hope and skepticism. "You two have a lot of work to do," she said, her voice firm. "But I see you trying. Don't let us down."

Antonio smiled, his respect for the elder woman evident. "We won't, Marta. We're committed to making this work."

Lea nodded in agreement. "We owe it to you all. We're not just fighting for ourselves anymore. We're fighting for the future of this community."

As they walked away, the sense of purpose and responsibility weighed heavily on their shoulders, but they were ready for the challenge. They knew that the road ahead would be difficult, but they were determined to lead the Cartel into a new era, one that honored the past while forging a better future.

The violent clash had left scars, but it had also opened the door to change. Antonio and Lea, united by their love and their shared vision, were ready to face whatever came next. Together, they would rebuild, restore, and redefine what it meant to be part of the Cartel, creating a legacy that would stand the test of time.

Chapter 18: New Beginnings

The morning sun filtered through the curtains of Lea's new apartment, casting a warm glow over the room. She sat at the small kitchen table, sipping her coffee and staring out the window at the bustling Miami streets below. The city was waking up, its pulse steady and familiar. Lea took a deep breath, savoring the moment of peace. It was a rare luxury in a life that had been anything but peaceful.

Lea's journey had been marked by hardship and danger, but also by resilience and strength. She had lost friends, family, and nearly lost herself in the violent world of the Cartel and The Get Money Girls. Yet, here she was, a survivor, standing at the precipice of a new chapter.

As she reflected on her past, memories flooded her mind. The pain of losing her cousin, the fierce battles she had fought, and the betrayal she had uncovered all played out like a movie reel. But with those memories came lessons learned. She had grown stronger, smarter, and more determined than ever to shape her own destiny.

Lea finished her coffee and stood, looking around her modest but comfortable apartment. It was a far cry from the opulence she had once known, but it was hers, and that meant everything. She had earned this fresh start, free from the shadows of her past.

The community outside had also begun to heal. The violent clash between the Cartel and The Get Money Girls had left its mark, but life moved on. People talked about the events in hushed tones, some remembering Lea's reign with a mix of fear and respect, while others chose to move past it, focusing on rebuilding and finding their own new beginnings.

Lea had made a conscious effort to reach out to the community, to show them that she was more than the leader of a deadly crew. She volunteered at local shelters, helped organize community events, and used her resources to support those in need. Slowly, she was rebuilding trust, not just in the community but also within herself.

Antonio had been a constant presence during this time, his unwavering support and love giving her the strength to continue. Their relationship had weathered storms that would have torn most couples apart, and they had emerged stronger, united by their shared experiences and a vision for a better future.

Lea's plans for the future were ambitious but grounded. She wanted to create a safe space for young women, offering them opportunities and support that she had never had. She envisioned a community center where girls could learn, grow, and find their own paths away from the lure of the streets. It was a way to honor her cousin's memory and to give back to the neighborhood that had shaped her.

One afternoon, as Lea was walking through the neighborhood, she ran into Marta. The elderly woman greeted her with a warm smile, her eyes twinkling with a mixture of curiosity and approval.

"Lea," Marta said, her voice firm but kind. "You've come a long way. I'm proud of you, child."

Lea felt a lump in her throat, the older woman's words touching a deep chord within her. "Thank you, Marta. That means a lot."

Marta nodded, her gaze steady. "Just remember, the streets never truly let go. Always watch your back."

Lea nodded, understanding the wisdom in Marta's words. The past had a way of lingering, and she knew she could never fully escape the life she had lived. But she was determined to keep moving forward, to build something positive out of the chaos.

Back at her apartment, Lea sat down at her desk, pulling out a notebook filled with plans and ideas for the community center. She spent hours working, her mind focused and her heart full of hope. This was her new beginning, a chance to make a difference and to leave a lasting legacy.

As the days turned into weeks and then months, Lea's vision began to take shape. The community center opened its doors, offering classes, counseling, and support to young women. It became a beacon of hope, a place where dreams could be nurtured and futures redefined.

Lea stood at the entrance of the center one evening, watching as a group of girls laughed and chatted, their faces filled with excitement and possibility. She smiled, feeling a deep sense of fulfillment. This was what she had fought for, what she had dreamed of during the darkest times.

Antonio joined her, slipping an arm around her waist. "Look at what you've built," he said softly, pride evident in his voice.

"We built this together," Lea replied, leaning into him. "I couldn't have done it without you."

They stood there for a moment, taking in the scene before them. The future was uncertain, and the shadows of their past would always be there, lurking at the edges. But for now, they had found a measure of peace, a new beginning that held the promise of brighter days.

Lea knew she would always need to watch her back, to stay vigilant. The streets never truly let go, and the life she had led had left its mark. But she was ready to face whatever came next, with Antonio by her side and a heart full of determination.

As the sun set over Miami, casting a golden glow over the city, Lea felt a sense of closure. Her journey had been tumultuous, filled with pain and loss, but it had also brought growth and new beginnings. She was at the top of her game, stronger and wiser, ready to embrace the future with open arms.

And as she stood there, watching the light fade and the stars begin to twinkle in the sky, Lea knew one thing for certain: she had found her place in the world, and she was ready to fight for it, no matter what challenges lay ahead.

Don't miss out!

Visit the website below and you can sign up to receive emails whenever Rachael Reed publishes a new book. There's no charge and no obligation.

https://books2read.com/r/B-A-WXARB-KOMPD

Connecting independent readers to independent writers.

Also by Rachael Reed

Codefendant
Codefendant
Once a Cheater
Once a Cheater
Passport Bro
What Happens in Prison
Preference
Sprinkle Sprinkle
Championship Bad
Street Exodus
Street Exodus
Street Royalty
Pawns of Power
SIS
Cartel Bloodline

Milton Keynes UK
Ingram Content Group UK Ltd.
UKHW040808160724
445389UK00004B/241